TO TIDDLES

First U.S. edition 2010

Library of Congress Cataloging-in-Publication Data

Voake, Charlotte.
Ginger and the mystery visitor / Charlotte Voake. — 1st U.S. ed.
p. cm.
Summary: Ginger and the small kitten are happy living with the little girl who looks after them
but one day a large and hungry visitor appears in the kitchen and licks out their bowls.
ISBN 978-0-7636-4865-7
[1. Cats—Fiction.] I. Title.
PZ7.V855Gm 2010
[E]—dc22   2009049505

10 11 12 13 14 15 16 LEO 10 9 8 7 6 5 4 3 2 1

Printed in Heshan, Guangdong, China

This book was typeset in Calligraphic 810.
The illustrations were done in watercolor and ink.

Candlewick Press
99 Dover Street
Somerville, Massachusetts 02144

visit us at www.candlewick.com

GINGER
and the mystery visitor

CANDLEWICK PRESS

Charlotte Voake

Ginger and the kitten
were very lucky cats.

They lived with
a little girl
who took very
good care of them.

Here she is,
giving them
breakfast . . .

a big bowl
for Ginger

and a little saucer
for the kitten.

But Ginger and the kitten
aren't the only ones
who like the look
of a nice
breakfast.

Someone
is watching them
through the
window!

"I wonder who that is," said the little girl, but nobody knew.

The visitor just stared
through the window,
watching Ginger
and the kitten
eat their
delicious meals.

Then one day,
they found him
in the kitchen,
licking out
their bowls.

When he had finished,
he gave himself
a wash . . .

and left!

Whenever the door
was open,
in he came.

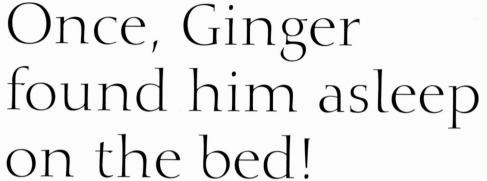

Once, Ginger
found him asleep
on the bed!

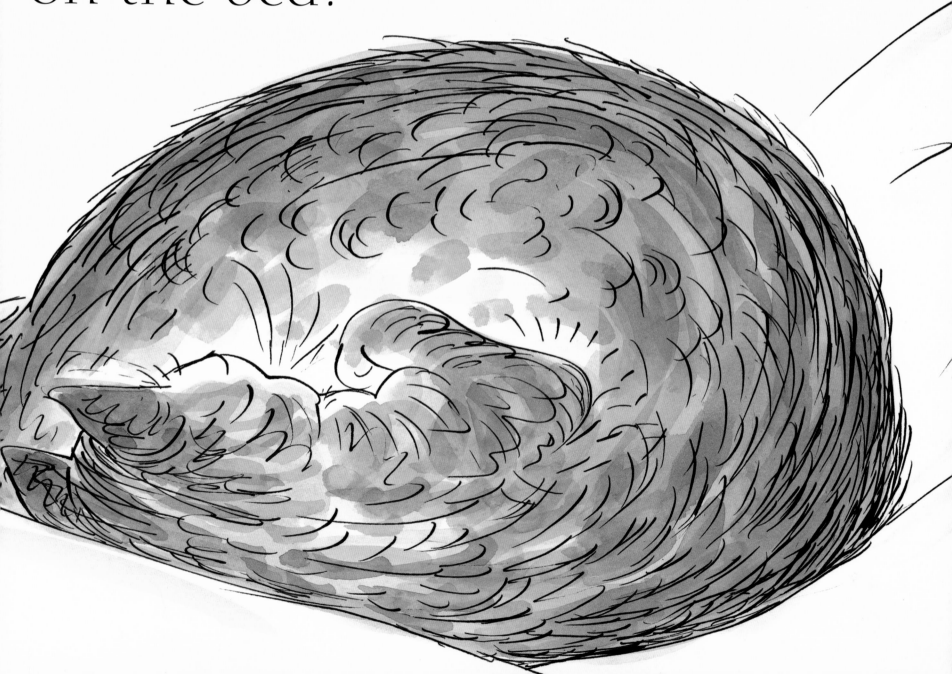

But the visitor never stayed long, and he never forgot to check the dishes on his way in or out.

"I wonder where
he comes from,"
said the little girl.
"I wonder where he goes.
I hope he's got someone nice
to look after him."

And then she had an idea.

She found
a piece of paper
and a bit
of ribbon,
and on the
paper
she wrote:

Do I
belong
to
anyone?

The next time
he visited,
she folded the
paper and tied
it around
his neck.

"Now we have
to wait,"
she said.

Ginger and the kitten had just finished eating supper when their visitor came to the window.

He looked
very
hungry.

He still
had the ribbon
around his neck.

But on the ribbon was a *different* piece of paper.

It was a reply, and this is what it said:

My name is Tiddles.
I have a loving
home and two square
meals a day.
Please do not
feed me as I
am getting
rather fat.

"TIDDLES?" said the little girl. "Tiddles, what a naughty little cat you are!"

Tiddles looked up at her.

"No, Tiddles," she said. "No more food for you!"

Tiddles just stared
hopefully
at the
empty dishes.

Poor Tiddles!
The little girl would not
let him in,
however sadly
he stared through the window.

"I'm sorry, Tiddles.
You have
a home of your own,"
she said.

Tiddles came to the window
less and less.

Then he stopped visiting
altogether.

But Ginger and the kitten
saw him quite often,

sometimes next door,
sometimes at the school
down the road . . .

up to his tricks
again.

"Here's our old friend!" everyone said, and Tiddles was very happy.

But wherever Tiddles visited,
he never stayed too long . . .

because, of course,
he had his own dinner
waiting for him . . .

at HOME!